Special thanks to Diane Reichenberger, Cindy Ledermann, Sarah Lazar, Charnita Belcher, Tanya Mann, Julia Phelps, Nicole Corse, Sharon Woloszyk, Rita Lichtwardt, Carla Alford, Renee Reeser Zelnick, Rob Hudnut, David Wiebe, Shelley Dvi-Vardhana, Gabrielle Miles, Rainmaker Entertainment, and Walter P. Martishius

Published in the United States by Golden Books, an imprint of Random House Children's Books, a division of Random House LLC, 1745 Broadway, New York, NY 10019, and in Canada by Random House of Canada Limited, Toronto, Penguin Random House Companies. No part of this book may be reproduced or copied in any form without permission from the copyright owner. Golden Books, A Golden Book, A Big Golden Book, the G colophon, and the distinctive gold spine are registered trademarks of Random House LLC.
randomhouse.com/kids
ISBN 978-0-385-38425-4 (trade) — ISBN 978-0-385-38426-1 (ebook)
Printed in the United States of America
10 9 8 7 6 5 4 3 2 1

Barbie AND THE SECRET DOOR

Adapted by Courtney Carbone

Based on the original screenplay by Brian Hohlfeld

Illustrated by Ulkutay Design Group

A GOLDEN BOOK • NEW YORK

Long ago, there was a very beautiful and very shy princess named Alexa. Instead of spending her time giving speeches, learning ballroom dances, and meeting royalty from faraway lands, all Alexa wanted to do was read. Her family tried to get her to come out of her shell.

"You can't hide from life forever, dear," Alexa's grandmother told her. "You'll never know what you're good at unless you try."

But Alexa preferred to sit on the sidelines with a book rather than be the center of attention.

One day, Alexa's grandmother gave her a special book.
"I've been saving this for the right time," she said.

The cover bore a picture of a magnificent door with glimmering swirls. The book told the story of a princess with magical powers. Alexa couldn't wait to read it! She thanked her grandmother and hurried outside, where she could read and daydream away from the pressures of palace life.

While Alexa was reading in the royal gardens, something in the distance caught her eye. It was a door she had never seen before, and it looked just like the one on the cover of her book! Mesmerized by the twirling, swirling colors, Alexa turned the knob and opened the door. . . .

She found herself traveling through a long, multicolored tunnel. With her heart racing, she followed the light and soon came upon a lush clearing filled with vibrant flowers and floating islands. It was like nothing she had ever seen!

Suddenly, an arrow flew toward her! Alexa jumped behind a hedge for cover, and the arrow hit the tree next to her. *Thunk!*

"You there!" a voice called. "Come out!"

Alexa slowly stepped out from the hedge and saw two girls. "I'm sorry," she said. "Maybe I should just go back the way I came."

"No, stay!" said one.

"Are you a princess?" asked the other. "You can help us!"

Alexa wondered how the girls knew she was a princess—until she noticed that her clothing had been transformed into an elaborate pink princess gown!

The girls introduced themselves as Nori and Romy. They told Alexa that she was in the kingdom of Zinnia, a magical land that fairies, mermaids, and unicorns had long called home.

Recently, the mean ten-year-old Princess Malucia had taken over the kingdom. Malucia was the only princess in Zinnia to be born without magical powers, so she was stealing magic from everyone.

"She took my magic and my wings," said the fairy Nori.

"She took my magic and my tail," Romy the mermaid added.

Soon everyone in Zinnia wanted to meet Alexa. They believed she had come to save them!

"I'm sorry to disappoint you, but I don't have any magic," Alexa said.

But her new friends laughed—there was a magic wand right in her hair! Alexa realized that her hair stick had turned into a beautiful wand with a glittering jewel on top!

Suddenly, the friends saw two strange-looking beasts coming up the path.

"Malucia's minions, the sniffers!" cried Nori. "They'll smell your magic!"

In an instant, three silk ropes dropped from the sky.

"Come on, Alexa!" Romy called, motioning for her to hold on to a rope. Alexa and Nori followed Romy's lead, and all three girls were whisked up into the treetops just in time.

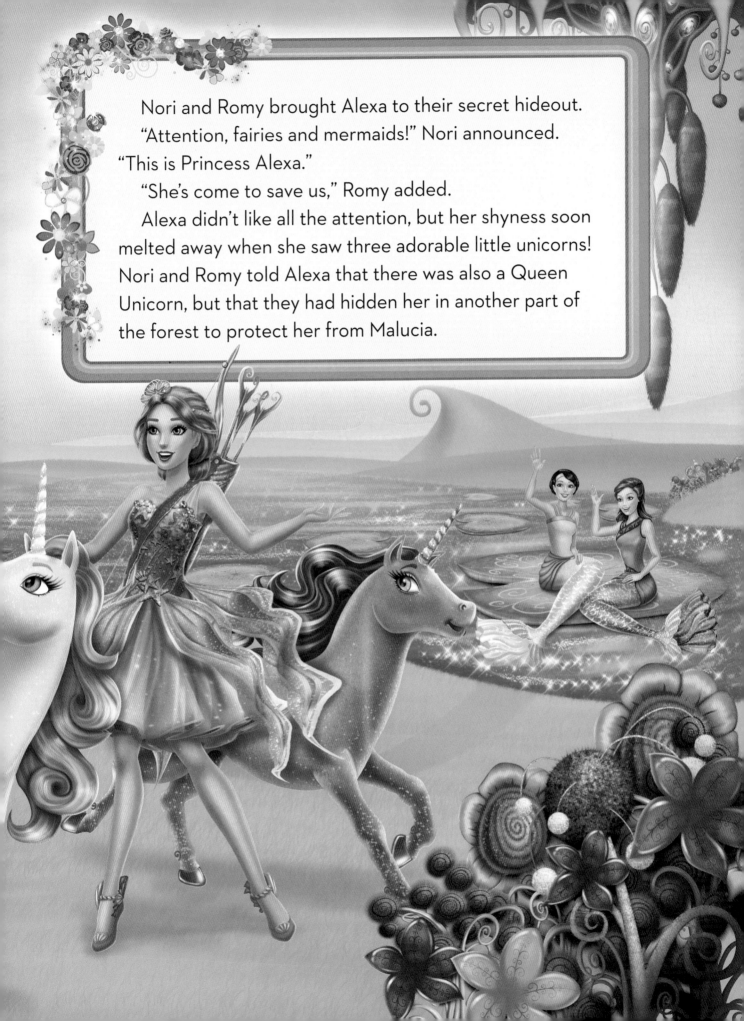

Nori and Romy brought Alexa to their secret hideout.

"Attention, fairies and mermaids!" Nori announced. "This is Princess Alexa."

"She's come to save us," Romy added.

Alexa didn't like all the attention, but her shyness soon melted away when she saw three adorable little unicorns! Nori and Romy told Alexa that there was also a Queen Unicorn, but that they had hidden her in another part of the forest to protect her from Malucia.

With Nori and Romy's help, Alexa tried out her magic. The princess waved her wand and transformed Nori's dress into the one Alexa had been wearing earlier! This new skill gave Alexa confidence and made her feel like a completely different person.

"With a princess on our side, we can fight Malucia and get our magic back," said Nori excitedly.

Meanwhile, at the castle, Malucia was planning a huge tea party to celebrate all the power she had stolen. As she was making her preparations, a set of her minions arrived with a youngling fairy named Nola in their clutches.

"You're no unicorn," Malucia said to Nola. "But you've got magic. And I want it!" The selfish girl pointed her scepter at the small creature and a yellowish-green light came streaming out. Malucia stole all of the fairy's magic, just as she had done to the other creatures in Zinnia.

Malucia's tea party was soon under way.

"So nice of all of you to join me for my magical tea party!" Malucia squealed.

"Did we have a choice?" one minion whispered to another.

"Don't talk to me unless you've found the unicorns!" she warned.

"What if we found the Queen Unicorn?" he asked. Malucia could not believe her good luck. The Queen Unicorn had been discovered in a magical grove.

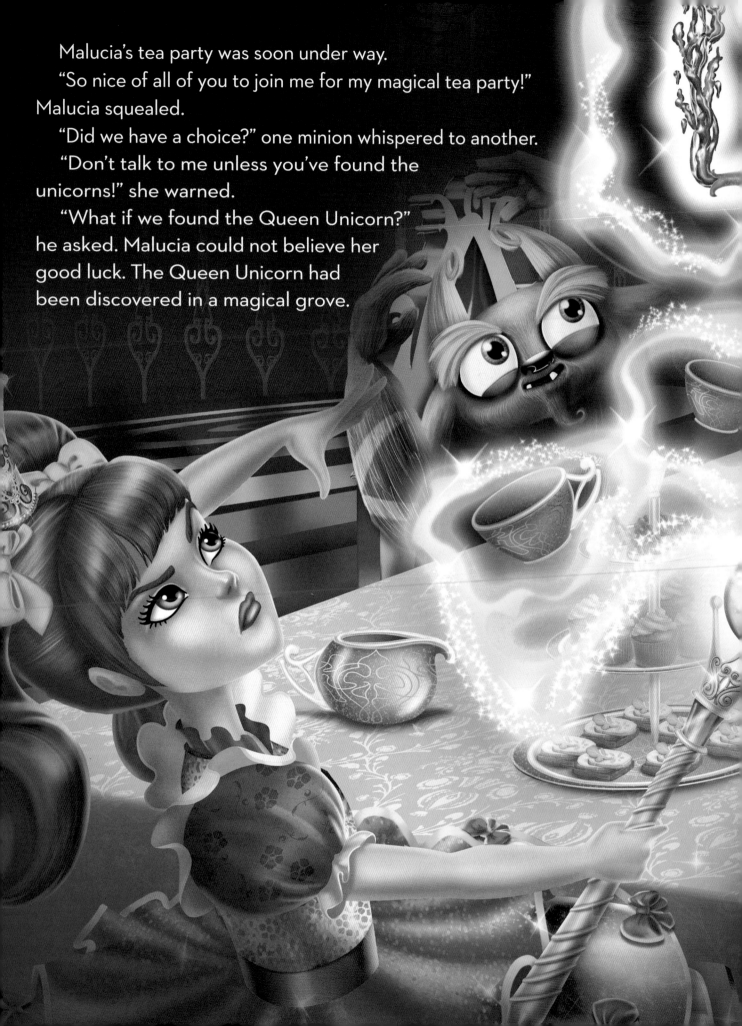

A sneaky plan crept into Malucia's mind. She would let Nola go free—and follow her back to the magical hideout! Soon, Malucia would have all the unicorn power in Zinnia!

Just as Malucia had hoped, the young fairy
ran back to the hideout to tell her friends what
had happened.

Alexa, Nori, and Romy knew they had to get to the Queen Unicorn as quickly as possible.

Alexa used her magical powers to create a flying carpet out of a lily pad! *"Woo!"* Nori exclaimed. It was like having wings again!

"This is so much fun!" Romy agreed.

The girls quickly made their way into a clearing and found the Queen Unicorn. She was the most amazing creature Alexa had ever seen! She was noble and majestic, with a long, flowing mane and a beautiful horn.

"We have to get you out of here!" Alexa told her. The Queen Unicorn nodded, allowing the three friends on her back. They quickly rushed to the secret hideout.

Unfortunately, Malucia and her minions were expecting them. "So I guess I'll take my unicorn," Malucia announced. "Put her in the cage!"

Alexa raised her wand, shooting a sparkling beam of light toward Malucia, but the mean princess fired a sickly green beam back at her. Alexa did everything she could to stop Malucia, but in all the confusion, her wand was broken. Malucia raced off with the unicorns.

Alexa promised to help her friends defeat Malucia. Suddenly, glittery sparkles appeared—and Alexa's wand was magically fixed!

Alexa, Nori, and Romy hurried to the castle, where they spied Malucia in her throne room. She drained all the magic from the Queen Unicorn, and its horn disappeared.

"Her scepter!" Nori cried. "It's starting to crack." Malucia's scepter could not handle all the power it contained. Alexa had a plan. She went inside the castle.

"Hey, Malucia! You want all the magic?" Alexa called. "Take it!"
Malucia pointed her scepter toward Alexa and began stealing her
princess magic. Suddenly, the scepter began to shake violently—
Malucia was losing control! At the last second, Alexa threw
her magic wand toward the glowing orb. It hit Malucia's
scepter right in the crack, causing it to explode!

Sparkling magic flowed from the scepter,
returning to everyone in the land. Alexa's outfit
transformed into a bright and shimmering ball
gown with glittering flowers. The fairies got back
their wings, the mermaids got back their tails, and
the unicorns got back their magical horns. Malucia
was defeated! Everyone cheered!
It had been a wonderful adventure, but Alexa knew it
was time to go home. She said good-bye to her new friends,
promising to come back and visit.

When Alexa got home, she surprised her parents by dancing at the royal ball. Alexa had become a stronger, braver person. There was simply too much to see and do to let fear get in the way of her dreams!

You never know what you can do until you try, Alexa thought as she danced with her friends. She smiled, ready for her next big adventure.